Sweet Revenge

Adapted by M. C. King

Based on the series created by Michael Poryes and Rich Correll & Barry O'Brien

Part One is based on the episode, "The Idol Side of Me," Written by Douglas Lieblein

Part Two is based on the episode, "Schooly Bully," Written by Douglas Lieblein & Heather Wordham

New York

Printed in the United States of America

First Edition
1 3 5 7 9 10 8 6 4 2

Library of Congress Control Number on file.
ISBN-13: 978-1-4231-0906-8
ISBN-10: 1-4231-0906-6

For more Disney Press fun, visit www.disneybooks.com
Visit DisneyChannel.com

Disney

HANNAH MONTANA

PART ONE

Chapter One

Everyone said Miley had to do it. *Singing with the Stars* was just about the most popular show on television. Plus, it was broadcast all over the world. So when the producers called to ask if Hannah Montana would be a special guest star, she couldn't say no.

Still, Miley had a funny feeling about it. *Singing with the Stars* matched regular people with famous people and had them perform together. Except Miley was both a regular person *and* a famous person. She was Miley Stewart, your average junior high school student. Then—with the help of wigs, makeup, and a totally awesome wardrobe—she was also Hannah Montana, teen superstar.

Singing with the Stars was a live show, and as Miley awaited her cue behind the screen, she half wished she had said no to appearing on it. Especially as she listened to host Bryan Winters trying to kill time and torture viewers by babbling on and on. Just get to the point already, dude! Miley thought. Tell us who's going home! Miley had met Bryan Winters when he was a smooth-talking deejay with his own morning radio show. He'd interviewed Hannah Montana a bunch of times. Now, he was a huge star, and he'd gone from smooth-talking to slime-talking. Miley groaned quietly to herself as he announced that the results were finally in, only to pause dramatically before saying he'd reveal them after the commercial break. What a tease.

"Well, there you have it, America!" Bryan told the crowd when the show came back after the commercial and he finally — *finally!* — revealed the winner. "Tonight, we saw Ethan Williams sing his heart out with Shakira and win his own recording contract. Give him a hand!" The audience roared while Ethan shook his hips à la Shakira. Miley knew the kid was psyched, but she couldn't help feeling a little embarrassed on his behalf. Leave the shaking to Shakira.

Watching it at home, Miley least enjoyed *Singing with the Stars* when Bryan sent the losing contestants home. Live, it was even more heartbreaking. The microphones made the contestants' sad sniffles sound like elephants wailing.

"Congratulations, Ethan, we'll see you after the show!" Bryan exclaimed. "Which means we have to say good-bye to these two adorable kids, who really have a fine career ahead of them as long as it doesn't involve singing."

Harsh, Miley thought, shaking her head. Bryan turned to face the despondent kids. "And I mean it, guys. Not even 'Happy Birthday.'" Whoa. Even harsher.

The stage manager whispered something into his headphones, then motioned to Miley. She was up next. She cleared her mind of all thoughts of losing contestants and obnoxious Bryan, then took a deep breath. Time to focus. She always did breathing exercises before performing onstage, and she knew how to tune out everything else.

"Next week on *Singing with the Stars*," Bryan told the audience, "three new hopefuls get their shot at a record deal by singing with *this* teen pop sensation. Who is she?"

The audience gasped in anticipation as the screen in front of Miley slowly rose. She stood completely still as the warm spotlight glowed around her. When the screen was all the way up, she grinned and struck a pose.

"Me! Hannah Montana!" Miley yelled in a way that managed to sound both perky and sincere. "See you all next week, and we'll really pump up the party!"

The audience roared as the producer signaled to roll the credits. The lights dimmed and a production assistant whisked Miley offstage—past Shakira and her entourage; past the winners and the losers who were clamoring for an autograph from Hannah Montana. Two burly security guards trailed them as they headed to stage door number three. Outside, a car was waiting to take Miley home. It was late, and she had to get to bed.

After all, she had school tomorrow.

Chapter Two

Only a few people knew Miley's secret identity. One of them was her best friend, Lilly Truscott. Through Hannah Montana, Lilly had met—or at least been in close proximity to—lots of celebrities. She'd hung in the green rooms of the biggest talk shows and the VIP lounges of the coolest clubs. Still, Lilly never got jaded or disillusioned. Miley appreciated that about her.

The two friends were in the school

cafeteria, which was as loud as a place could be, but Lilly made sure to whisper. "I can't believe you're gonna be the celebrity singer on *Singing with the Stars*," she gushed. "That makes Hannah Montana just about the coolest person ever!"

Miley and Lilly chose two seats at a random table and plunked their trays down. They hadn't even picked up their hot dogs when the strangest thing happened: within seconds of their arrival, everyone else at the table got up and left without saying a word. And not because they all had class. They simply moved to another table!

Huh?

Miley and Lilly looked at each other in confounded shock. Then, since they were best friends, who often were thinking the exact same thing at the exact same time, they bent their heads toward their underarms in unison thinking: *Uh-oh! I stink!*

Did I forget to shower? Miley wondered in horror. It had been very hot in the studio last night. Especially with all that makeup. She *had* been sweaty. She scrunched up her nose, prepared herself for the worst, and took a whiff. *Hmm.* She took another whiff just to be safe. *Phew!* It wasn't her. She smelled like the powder-fresh deodorant she kept hidden in the back of the bathroom drawer so her older brother Jackson wouldn't use it when he ran out of his.

Meanwhile, Lilly had gotten similarly positive sniff-test results. "Must be you," they accused each other.

Just then, Oliver Oken approached their table. He was Miley and Lilly's second best friend, and the only other person at school who knew Miley's secret. Oliver looked furtively around the room, as if trying to gauge how much trouble he'd be in if he took a seat. "Uh, guys, bad news," he muttered, shaking his head in dismay. He held a thick wad of paper, which he handed Lilly. "Amber and Ashley's annual cool list is out again."

Miley and Lilly exchanged a look as if to say, "Duh! Should have known!"

"Well, that explains it," Miley said, glancing at the first page. Amber and Ashley were the most competitive girls at school. And they had it in for Miley and Lilly.

"How far down did they put us this year?" Lilly asked. She and Miley scanned the list.

They weren't on the first page.

Or the second.

Or the third.

"Keep going . . . keep going . . . keep—"
Oliver instructed. They kept going until it
was just too painful. Oliver couldn't take it
anymore! "Just skip to the last page," he
said finally.

"Wow!" Miley exclaimed. "We're tied
for dead last with Dandruff Danny."

Dandruff Danny happened to be nearby.
At the sound of his name, he stopped
scratching his head momentarily to look up
and ask, "Is someone actually talking to
me?" You could hear the hope and desper-
ation in his voice.

That was Oliver's cue. Talking to
Dandruff Danny could *really* damage his
standing on the list! "Okay, see you later."

"Where are you going?" Miley asked.
Lunch period had just started.

"Look," Oliver replied, "I finally cracked
the top one hundred." And then, because

two jocks were passing by, he raised his voice to make sure they heard. "No way I'm talking to people from the last page." Miley and Lilly just stared at him. "Stop begging," he said even louder, though Miley and Lilly hadn't made a peep. Then, when he was sure the jocks were out of earshot, he whispered apologetically, "I'll see you after dark." Then he scurried off.

Miley was originally from Tennessee, and so she had a tendency to whip out phrases that no one in California understood. As she watched Oliver ditch them for a top—one hundred table, she remarked, "That boy flip-flops more than a catfish in a moon bouncer."

Lilly would have said "*What?!*" only she didn't have a chance. Seconds later, Amber, Ashley, and a group of followers were hovering nearby, with Amber eyeing them as if they were caged animals at the zoo. "Look, everyone," she told the group. "It's a couple of last-page losers in their native habitat." By native habitat, she meant the empty cafeteria table.

"So sad," Ashley said, faking a sad expression. "Still eating. As if they had a reason to live."

That was it! Miley had had enough! She was about to tell Amber and Ashley what she thought of their stupid list *and* what they could do with it . . . but they were even quicker than Oliver. A couple of nasty remarks and—*poof!*—they had moved on, taking their pathetic group of followers with them.

Well, so what? There were other people who needed to hear what she had to say. Miley rose from her seat. "Listen!" she yelled in the voice she usually reserved for screaming at Jackson. "This list is as bogus as the people who wrote it."

She looked around. No one was listening. She figured maybe they couldn't hear her, so she climbed on a chair. "Come on, everybody! Let's show Amber and Ashley they can't tell us who's cool and who's not! Let's rip up these lists right now!"

With as much dramatic flair as possible, Miley tore the first page in half. She listened for the collective ripping sound of hundreds of pages tearing. Instead, all she heard was Lilly.

"Miley?"

Miley opened her eyes. "I'm the only one doing it, aren't I?" she said. Her shoulders sagged in defeat.

A lone voice called out to her. "I'm with ya, sister!" It was Dandruff Danny, holding up his list in triumphant solidarity. He made a valiant attempt to rip the first page in half. Sadly, he didn't have the strength.

Chapter Three

Miley wasn't giving up. She had to get the word out: Amber and Ashley's list was bogus. Not only that, it was mean. They went to a big school—surely, there were kids out there who agreed with her.

Hanging in the hallway between classes, she and Lilly discussed the topic at hand. "Okay," Miley conceded, "so some people do care about the list. But there are plenty of other decent people, strong enough to think for themselves, and those are the people I want for my friends anyway."

Speaking of which! Miley looked up to see Sarah from her science class standing against her locker. Sarah! Sarah was supernice. She often volunteered at the old age home up the street. She worked at a soup kitchen on weekends. Plus, she was sweet and funny. She was always making Miley crack up during lab. Sarah wouldn't be into the list, no way! She had too much integrity.

"Hi, Sarah!" Miley called out. What a relief to find someone else who still had her senses.

"Oh, hi, guys," Sarah said, shuffling awkwardly from side to side. "Listen, Miley, I'm really sorry, but I can't be your lab partner. Today after school I have to read to the blind, serve punch at a blood drive, and hose out cages at the animal shelter."

Miley knew Sarah was charitable, but that sure sounded like a lot to do. Something wasn't right.

"Wait a minute," Miley said as Sarah tried to duck away. "You read to the blind yesterday."

"I, uh, took an extra shift," Sarah explained. She stared down at her sneakers.

"Extra shift, my Aunt Petunia!" Miley cried. The words shot rapid-fire out of Miley's mouth. "You're bailing on me because I'm last on Amber and Ashley's list. Aren't you?"

"No, I'm not," Sarah answered, sounding not at all convincing. She looked up from her sneakers, then off to the side . . . anywhere as long as she wouldn't catch Miley's angry glare. Then she caught sight of something that made her face fill with panic.

"Oh, no, here comes Amber," she said with a shudder. "Sorry," she mumbled. This time she sounded like she almost meant it. "I'm charitable, not stupid."

Lilly and Miley watched in disbelief as yet another person tore away from them in terror. "Hey, even Saint Sarah is freezing us out!" Lilly remarked.

Across the hall, list co-author Amber was dealing with her own drama as a tearful classmate pleaded despairingly. "But Amber, you have to come to my party! It'll be a total disaster without you."

Miley and Lilly cringed. Why did Amber wield so much power?

"That is so true," Amber nodded in agreement. "But my mom let me audition for *Singing with the Stars,* and if they have any taste, I'll be singing with Hannah Montana Saturday night."

Had Miley and Lilly heard right? Amber and Hannah Montana in a duet on *Singing with the Stars*?

"Okay, I have to run to the bathroom," Amber told the girl. "I haven't looked at myself in, like, a half hour."

Miley didn't know what to feel first: horror that she might be sharing a stage with Amber or excited that maybe this was her chance to turn things around. Miley wasn't a diva, but she could probably voice her opinion if she didn't like the contestant she was matched with.

"Okay," she said to Lilly, "maybe we can't get rid of that stupid list, but I can make darn sure Amber never gets to sing with Hannah Montana."

Lilly nodded vigorously. It sounded like

the perfect plan to her.

Just then, the door to the girls bathroom swung open and the most horrific sound came pouring out. Had the electric hand dryers gone on the fritz again? Had yet another frustrated member of the marching band flushed her flute down the toilet?

Then the sound became more than an infernal howl. It became a song. Or at least a sad attempt at a song. A sad attempt at a *Hannah Montana* song, the one she'd be performing on Saturday's show!

Miley and Lilly watched as a girl ran out of the bathroom covering her ears. They couldn't believe it! That horrible howl must be coming from . . . Amber.

There were often contestants on *Singing with the Stars* who acted as if they were the next Christina Aguilera, yet couldn't hit a note. Miley always wondered how it was that someone could be so deluded. And why wasn't anyone in the contestants' lives kind enough to tell them the truth? Now she finally understood!

She had to rework her plan. If she used her pull to get Amber off *Singing with the Stars*, she'd be doing Amber a favor. Better to let her humiliate herself! She'd have to make sure Amber got *on* the show.

"You could do that?" Lilly sounded impressed.

"Sometimes you gotta fight fire with fire," Miley said. "She likes to make fun of people. Well, I'm gonna make sure she knows what it feels like."

"Oh, boy!" Lilly could barely contain herself. This plan was just *too* awesome! "Once the world hears her sing, she'll be on the bottom of her own stupid list."

They could only hope. . . .

Chapter Four

If Hannah Montana was going to record a new album in the near future, she had to have some new songs. That meant Robby Stewart, her dad and manager, had to get some writing done.

He'd set aside the entire afternoon to be alone with his guitar. Now all he needed was some peace, quiet, and inspiration. He already had a first line. Well, the first half of a line. He couldn't figure out the last word. He sang the words he'd written so far—

Awoooooooooo!

He tried again —

Awooooooooooo!

Like Miley, Mr. Stewart loved all animals. Still, he would have appreciated it if his next door neighbor's dog, Oscar, shut his yap just this once. Too bad Oscar's owner was Mr. Dontzig, a man with a bad attitude and a grudge against the Stewart family. Something about overgrown hedges . . .

"Hey, Dontzig!" Mr. Stewart shouted as he walked outside. "Can you ask your dog to keep his opinions to himself?"

"Oh, is Oscar bothering you, Stewart?" Mr. Dontzig sounded friendly enough.

"Yes!"

"Good boy, Oscar!"

So much for friendly! And so much for peace and quiet. . . .

❖ ❖ ❖

When Jackson got home from school, he found his father frustrated and despairing. He decided to take matters into his own hands. After all, he liked a challenge. And as a bonus, he could make his old man proud.

Mr. Stewart said he didn't want to know how Jackson was going to get Oscar to quiet down; he just wanted him to do it. So Mr. Stewart closed his ears and shut his eyes to the clanging from the kitchen and the slamming of doors. He heard Jackson's footsteps on the walkway, then some barking. Then it was silent—eerily so.

"Well, I finally got that dog to stop barking," Jackson announced when he returned. "Just took that big T-bone from the fridge and chucked it over the fence."

Mr. Stewart replayed the words in his head. That. Big. T-bone. Is that really what his beloved son had just said? *Argh!*

"You mean the one that I dry-rubbed, tenderized, and marinated for forty-eight hours?" he asked in disbelief.

Poor Jackson. He'd only been trying to help! "No, the other one?" he said weakly, desperate to dodge the moment of truth.

"Jackson Rod Stewart! I cook, I clean, I work my fingers to the bone, and what's my reward?"

There was a knock at the door. Mr. Stewart answered it to discover a smug Mr. Dontzig holding Oscar in his arms. And there was Mr. Stewart's prized T-bone, ensnared in the tiny dog's gnarly teeth.

"Hello, Stewarts. Oscar wanted to thank you for the T-bone. Oh, and next time, he'd like a twice-baked potato on the side. No sour cream, that gives him gas."

Mr. Stewart narrowed his eyes as Mr. Dontzig gloated. This was war. . . .

Chapter Five

That night, after a sorry dinner of soggy leftovers and no steak, Mr. Stewart ambled outside. Maybe a walk would be good for thinking up lyrics.

He was surprised to find Jackson on the deck. He'd rigged up a sound system, complete with sound board and microphone. What was going on now?

"Check it out," Jackson said proudly. "I set up some of Hannah's concert speakers in Dontzig's hedge. Next time that dog barks, he's gonna find out my woofer's bigger than his."

Mr. Stewart had to hand it to his son: the kid had gumption. "You actually think this might work?"

Awoooooooooo! Apparently Oscar was out for a nightly stroll as well.

"Only one way to find out," Jackson replied. "Would you like to do the honors?"

Mr. Stewart had to admit it sounded like fun. He took the microphone from his son. "Don't mind if I do," he said.

He cleared his throat, stared at the moon, and howled the biggest, baddest dog howl he could muster. *Awoooooooooo!*

Silence.

They did it! Mr. Stewart slapped Jackson's shoulder in congratulations. They high-fived and grinned at each other.

Finally! He could get back to his music.

But then Jackson saw something. His face fell. "What's that little rat doing now?"

Mr. Stewart craned his neck to see.

"Hey!" Jackson called. "Get away from those speakers! Put your leg down. Put your—"

Sparks flew from the speakers as the lights from the Stewarts' house flickered. There was an ominous *pop!*, then the speakers shorted and the fuse blew, followed by one blissful moment of silence. Then Oscar started barking again. This time he was joined by all the other dogs on the block.

So much for a pleasant walk. And so much for writing lyrics. Mr. Stewart had to go inside to call the electric company.

Chapter Six

Miley and Lilly tried to convince themselves they weren't outcasts. They tried to convince themselves that even if they were outcasts, it didn't matter. They wouldn't want to spend their lives sucking up to Amber and Ashley anyway!

Still, back at their lunch table, alone again, it was hard for Miley and Lilly not to feel the sting of being labeled losers. Across the way, Amber and Ashley's table buzzed with energy and excitement. A guy in a football-letter jacket carried a tray holding two cans of diet soda. He plunked it in front of the girls as if he were a waiter in a fancy restaurant. A girl gave Ashley a shoulder massage. And was there someone kneeling by Amber's feet?! Miley couldn't believe her eyes. Was Amber getting a pedicure? In the cafeteria? Suddenly, Miley wasn't very hungry anymore.

Having decided to put Operation: Humiliate Amber into motion at *Singing with the Stars*, Miley had given up on her campaign to woo other students away from the dark side. She'd even given up on Oliver, who was secretly calling her every night to chat. She was fine letting him have his moment in the sun. She didn't even flinch when he walked by their table with a group of guys who wouldn't have acknowledged his existence before he cracked the top one hundred.

"Ah! Cramp!" Oliver cried, clutching his knee, and dramatically jumping up and down. "Must've worked out too hard last night," he told the guys. "Just go on without me."

He leaned into Miley and Lilly's table and waited until his newfound friends had moved out of earshot. "I miss you guys!" he whispered.

Lilly said, "Listen, Oliver—"

"Don't look at me when you talk!" he cried in a panic. He turned away from them and spoke softly out of the corner of his mouth, "So, have you talked to the producers yet? Are they actually gonna let Amber be on the show?"

"If you're not going to look at us, we're not going to tell you," Lilly snapped.

She was feeling less tolerant than Miley.

"Yeah, and it's really good," Miley teased.

Oliver strained to move his head toward them. But it was as if a powerful force held it in place.

"Oliver!" Lilly yelled.

Finally, he turned to face them. Miley ignored the pained expression on his face and told him the latest on Amber. "Not only is she on the show, guess who gets to give her the good news?" She didn't wait for Oliver to guess, because an idea suddenly dawned on her: no time like the present! She whipped out her cell phone, and started to dial.

Oliver's features relaxed, and he began to smile. "Okay, this is so worth it!" Boy, was he stoked!

"I know," Miley said, glancing at

Amber's crowded table. Everyone was eating. "I'm just waiting for the right mouthful of pasta salad. . . ." She watched as Amber heaved a loaded fork toward her glossy lips. "Ooh, that's a good one!" Miley had already keyed in the numbers. With a gleeful flick of her finger, she hit SEND.

Leave it to Amber to have the most obnoxiously loud cell-phone ring! Of course she wouldn't care about noise pollution! As soon as Amber answered, Miley ducked behind Oliver and Lilly.

"Hello?" Amber said through a mouth of gooey pasta.

Miley took a deep breath. It was just a phone call, but it still required focus. "Hi, Amber," she said in her most professional voice. "It's Hannah Montana."

Amber was so shocked, she spat her mouthful of food across the table. Miley could hear Ashley's horrified cry of "Gross!" in stereo — both through the phone and across the room.

Ha! Miley couldn't have been more pleased with how this was going. "The producers asked me to call and tell you that you're one of the three lucky people performing with me on *Singing with the Stars*!"

Amber had taken a swig of fruit punch to wash down the sticky pasta. Now she spit that out, too. Miley peeked from behind her friends just as the red spray hit Ashley in the face.

Nice shot! she almost said out loud, then stopped herself. *Phew.*

"Anyhoo," Miley went on, "they'll call you with the *deets.* I can't wait to meet you."

"Thank you! Thank you so much!" Amber cried. Miley had never heard Amber be so polite.

"Don't be silly, you deserve everything you're gonna get. Bye." Miley hit END, smiling slyly as Amber rose to her feet in jubilation.

"Hey, everybody!" she hollered. "I'm going to be singing with Hannah Montana on *Singing with the Stars*!"

Even Miley, Lilly, and Oliver joined in the cheering. After all, they had something to celebrate, too.

"Who wants to hear the song I'm going to sing on the show?" Amber asked the crowd.

"I think we all do!" Ashley cried.

This was going to be easier than Miley thought! She didn't even have to wait until Saturday for Amber to humiliate herself. Amber was going to do it right here, right now, in front of everyone. Miley, Lilly, and Oliver cheered even louder.

"Well, if you insist," Amber said, gearing up to sing. Miley braced herself.

But to Miley's surprise, the most unexpected sound came out of Amber's mouth. She was singing—beautifully. Where was the infernal howl? The off-key, tone-deaf wailing? The Amber they'd heard in the bathroom? Something was wrong! Amber sounded . . . amazing.

Lilly looked just as dumbfounded. "But she—"

"Her voice—" Miley sputtered.

Oliver looked flabbergasted. "You said—" Miley and Lilly had no response. Oliver pressed: "Then who did you guys hear in the bathroom?"

That's when Ashley decided to join in the singing. As she wailed away, Miley and Lilly looked at each other and winced. Mystery solved. *Ashley*—not Amber—

was the Infernal Howler! They hadn't realized she'd been in the bathroom, too.

Now what were they going to do? If there was a bright side to all this, Miley couldn't see it.

Chapter Seven

The big day had finally arrived. Miley had spent the afternoon in wardrobe, and she was pleased with the results: dark jeans, cute boots, awesome blouse. In general, she preferred Miley's low-maintenance, casual beach duds to Hannah Montana's rock-and-roll chic. Still, it was fun to have stylists make you look like a pop superstar. More important, dressing the part helped get her into the

Hannah Montana mind-set she needed to be in to perform.

At least that's *usually* how it was. Now, as hard as she tried, Miley couldn't get her mind off her real-life problem: Amber. She, Lilly, and Oliver had traded calls and e-mails all night, yet they still hadn't come up with a way to put Amber in her place. Boy, did Miley regret securing her a spot on that night's show. She was obviously going to win, which meant she'd become a total diva—or an even bigger diva than she already was—and make Miley and Lilly's life at school even more *miserable*!

Argh!

Miley stood onstage, rehearsing the very song she'd heard Ashley destroy in the cafeteria.

Just then, a stage manager approached, holding a clipboard. In her many years in the business, Miley had met lots of stage managers and they were always the same: straight, to the point, and in a rush. The guy from *Singing with the Stars* was no different. He cut her off midverse. "That's great, Hannah," he said, checking the production schedule. "And after that you'll hug . . ." He consulted the day's call sheet. ". . . Amber Addison."

Amber. Addison. Hearing her name come out of the stage manager's mouth made it sound so official. This was really happening. The stage manager continued giving her the show rundown. "Bryan will say something he thinks is funny — try to laugh, it'll be over before you know it."

That's what you think, bub, Miley thought.

✼ ✼ ✼

Lilly accompanied Miley to all of Hannah Montana's concerts dressed as Lola Luftnagle, a purple-wigged, vintage clothes—wearing member of Hannah's entourage. Lilly was a self-proclaimed *Singing with the Stars* addict, and being on set just before the live show started was making her a little loopy. When the stage manager had gone, Lilly practically bounded onto the stage.

"Look!" she cried, pointing to a suspiciously shiny spot on the floor. "This must be where the losers stand. There are puddle stains from all the drippy, nervous sweat." She gazed at the icky spot on the floor as if she were at the Louvre in Paris and had just spotted the *Mona Lisa* for the first time.

"Lilly!" Miley wanted to scream, but she was careful not to break from character in public. "Lola!" she yelled instead. "Would you please focus? Amber's got a real shot at winning this. And if she does, that list will be the least of our problems."

Lilly looked up from the floor and furrowed her brow in consternation. "We've got to do something."

"Ya think?" Miley quipped sarcastically. Here they were with minutes until the live show began airing, and they didn't have a plan!

Two explosions of smoke rose from either side of the stage.

"Whoa! That is so cool," Lilly gushed. "What is it?"

"The beginning of the end," Miley said with a groan. The stage manager had told her they'd be doing one more smoke rehearsal, then the audience would enter and the show would start.

She explained to Lilly, "We enter through

the smoke, then Amber sings great and you and I are on the bottom of the cool list till we're seniors." And because that wasn't dramatic enough, she added, "And I'm talking blue-haired, bingo-playing, mitten-knitting seniors."

Lilly had a funny look in her eye. "Maybe . . . and maybe not."

"What are you up to?" Miley was a little nervous. Lilly's plans could be pretty far-fetched, and here they were without a second to spare! There was no time for mistakes.

"Remember my exploding volcano disaster at last year's science fair?" Lilly asked.

How could Miley forget? Lilly's science project was the talk of the school for months. It was the biggest disaster to hit the school since Florence Fishman dyed her hair green and then got a Mohawk!

"Mt. Saint Lilly?" Miley recalled. "People were blowing lava out of their noses for a week."

"Well, if I could do that by accident," Lilly added devilishly, "imagine what I can do to Amber on purpose."

Miley remembered how the black gunk had dripped from their science teacher's bushy eyebrows; how gray clouds had filled the auditorium; how soot had rained on the cheerleaders' brand-new uniforms and clogged the marching band's instruments; and how it had gotten under everybody's fingernails. And then there was the smell! A combination of superglue and Magic Marker with a distinctive eau de wet dog . . . Ah, good times.

"I'm imagining . . ." Miley said as she envisioned a slide show of Amber in varying stages of hideousness. Things were starting to look up again! ". . . and I'm liking it!"

A plan! And just in the nick of time. . . .

Chapter Eight

Miley had to admit it—Lilly had really come through for her this time. While Miley was getting miked by the sound guy and having her Hannah wig fixed by the hair guy, Lilly had worked out a surefire plot to sabotage Amber's performance. There were two entrances to the stage—one with green smoke, one with red. The green one was rigged to give Amber a makeover. All Miley had to do was convince her to go through it.

Luckily, the stage manager had asked Miley and Lilly to wait in a spot backstage that provided a perfect vantage point for seeing Amber's dressing room. No surprise: Ashley was with her.

"Go ahead, primp all you want, Little Miss Cool List," Lilly mocked. "You're about to have a makeup malfunction people will be downloading forever."

"She won't get hurt or anything, right?" Miley asked.

Lilly shook her head. "Just her pride, nationwide, nowhere to hide, humilified, sad inside—" When she got overexcited, Lilly had a tendency to rhyme.

"Are you done?" Miley asked.

Lilly nodded. "Just remember, you go through the red. She goes through the green, because she's mean, like an evil queen—"

Miley glared. Lilly cut the rhymes.

"How do I look?" Miley heard Amber ask Ashley with an uncharacteristic tremble in her voice.

"Like a star!" Ashley answered. Miley had to hand it to Ashley: that was the right supportive-friend thing to say. Except Ashley kept going.

"I can't believe you're about to sing in front of thirty million people," she added. "And that's just America. There's Canada and Europe and the Soviet Reunion—"

The Soviet Reunion? Miley thought. Boy, *someone* wasn't paying attention during Mr. Lambert's history class.

"Forget the fact that it's live," Ashley continued. "Forget that if you screw up, everyone in the whole world will be laughing at you. Just put that out of your head."

Wow, Ashley had a funny way of being supportive! And poor Amber barely had the strength to fight back. "It wasn't in my head," she said through gritted teeth. "Until now."

"Oops. My bad," Ashley chirped. "Have a good show."

Miley couldn't help it. A wave of sympathy overtook her. Amber looked so nervous! Still, it was time to get the plan underway, so she pushed the feelings to the back of her mind. When Lilly nudged her, she took a deep breath and left her spot in the wings.

"Hey, Amber!" she called out. "Y'all ready for your big number?"

At the sight of Hannah Montana—*the* Hannah Montana—Amber dodged out of sight. Miley followed her.

"Hannah, I can't do this!" Amber cried. "I can't go out there."

Miley saw the fear in the poor girl's eyes and steeled herself to resist her more compassionate urges. This is Amber, she reminded herself. Cruel, heartless, have-no-mercy, list-making Amber.

"Hey," Miley said. "Everything is going to be fine as long as you go through the green arch. I repeat, the green arch." She pointed Amber toward it.

But Amber didn't want to go on at all. "No, no," she faltered. "I'm gonna screw up. I know I'm gonna screw up."

This was going to be harder than Miley thought.

"Listen, sometimes I have these worries, too. And you know what two words always get me through it: green arch. See ya out there!" she called, turning to leave.

Except Amber still stood frozen in place. She didn't make a move for the green arch.

"Come on," Miley coaxed. Oh, this was bad. "Get into position. Gonna be a blast."

"You don't understand." Amber was

practically bawling now. "I can't be made fun of again."

"Again?" What was she talking about? Stage fright was one thing, but had Amber completely lost it? "When has anyone made fun of you?" Miley *had* to hear this.

"Well, I know it's hard to believe, looking at how beautiful I am now . . ." Amber was being earnest here. ". . . but when I was a kid, I was the geeky girl with glasses. The one that everyone teased all the time."

No way! "Really? How geeky? Wouldn't happen to have any pictures, would you?"

Oops! Miley realized that she sounded a little too interested. "You know," she scrambled to cover. "It'll help me feel the pain."

Amber looked forlorn. "No, I burned them all. And I'm always afraid it's going to happen again."

Miley had watched enough Oprah and

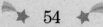

Dr. Phil to know where this was going. "So you make fun of people now because of what people did to you when you were a geeky little kid?"

"Yes," Amber confessed. "Yes, I do."

"But you shouldn't do that. Don't you get it? When you fight fire with fire—"

Uh-oh. Something suddenly dawned on Miley. "All you get is a bigger fire," she said.

"I know," Amber answered sadly. "Now I'm gonna flame out in front of America, Asia, and the Soviet Reunion."

Apparently someone *else* hadn't been paying attention in history class. "You mean, Russia?" Miley gently corrected.

"Ah, man, we're on there, too?!" Amber wailed.

Miley was still thinking about fighting fire with fire, and how, if she was going to live up to her own words, she would have to put her own torch down. Lilly was not going to like this!

"Look, if I could promise that you would look great out there, would you promise me that you will be a better person?"

"Yeah," Amber didn't hesitate to reply. "But could you really make that happen?"

"I can pretty much guarantee you'll come out looking better than me," Miley said.

The stage manager called for places.

"Oh, no!" Amber gasped.

"You're gonna be fine. Just . . ." Miley paused, unsure of herself for a second. Was she really going to do what she was about to do? "Just enter through the red arch," she finished.

"But you said green," Amber reminded her.

"And now I'm saying red. Look, just do it before I change my mind. And remember . . . better person."

Chapter Nine

"**A**nd we're back with our final contestant," announced Bryan Winters, aiming his bright grin at the camera. "From Malibu, California, give it up for Amber Addison!"

As the crowd cheered and the puffs of smoke erupted, he gestured toward the green arch—where the contestants usually made their entrances. Miley couldn't say she didn't enjoy watching Bryan fumble as Amber emerged from the red arch instead.

Still, she felt a little bad for the stage manager who'd worked so hard to make sure everything went off without a hitch. She'd have to remember to send him a really nice thank-you gift.

Hitting the stage, Amber did look slightly stricken, and Miley wondered if her new plan was going to be a total bust. But then the orchestra started and the lights dimmed. The crowd's attention seemed to embolden Amber. She sang even better than she had in the cafeteria.

That was Miley's cue. Here goes nothing, she thought, as she stood before the green arch. Please don't work! Please don't work! Miley begged as she began her walk of doom.

But her pleading didn't work. Miley made her entrance, coughing green powder, her wig a wild frizz. The audience gasped: their beloved Hannah Montana had turned into a green and dusty Frankenstein!

Ever the pro, Miley tried to play it cool, singing along with Amber. But with every word, her throat got more clogged with powder and smoke. She did her best to focus as she struggled to breathe. She used all her mental powers to concentrate on not coughing. Keep going! she told herself. You can do it.

Except she couldn't. The itchiness in her throat! The powder in her nose! She couldn't sing another note. Miley leaned forward and let the coughing fit get the better of her.

What was happening? The audience looked baffled as the stage manager whispered into his walkie-talkie, telling the cameras to cut away from Hannah Montana and focus on Amber.

And Amber, who had just been so scared a few minutes ago, seized the moment, belting out the song with even more soul than before. So much for stage fright!

Miley tried to recover. She started to sing, but could only gasp for air. She was feeling faint. Desperate, she reached out for something solid to hold on to. The only thing was a hollow plaster pillar—meant only as a prop. As Miley leaned on it, the pillar collapsed, propelling her into the air and offstage.

Lilly ran to her side. "I may have used a little too much green," she admitted.

Chapter Ten

For the first time in what seemed like forever, Oliver didn't look nervously from side to side before taking a seat at the "outcast" table. "I've been thinking about it, and I don't care what anybody else says, you're my real friends," he announced. "I'm sitting with you."

As weaselly as he'd been behaving, Miley couldn't hold a grudge. She reached over to hug him.

"Careful, green bean, you're showing," Lilly warned, pointing to Miley's arm. Even after twenty showers, four different brands of exfoliant, and six bars of soap, Miley's skin was still tinged green. On the upside, she smelled like a delicious blend of lemon verbena, French vanilla, and Hawaiian papaya and guava.

"What are you gonna do now?" Oliver asked. "Not only did Amber win, she's gonna get a recording contract."

"All because you had to be a good person." Lilly sighed. "I hate when you do that!"

Miley was still holding out the hope that Amber had taken Hannah Montana's words to heart. "Don't worry, it's all gonna be worth it. Trust me."

The cafeteria erupted in hoots and hollers when Amber and Ashley finally showed. This is it, thought Miley, crossing her fingers. Amber shushed the crowd. It was time for her big announcement.

"As you all know," she said dramatically, "last night I was the big winner. But before that happened, I made a promise to myself and to my new best friend, Hannah Montana."

Adios, outcast table! Miley thought to herself.

Amber continued. "So I'm doing something really drastic to the list."

You're going to rip it up for good! Miley was practically giddy.

". . . Dandruff Danny, you and your flakes are ahead of . . ." Amber pointed at Miley and Lilly. ". . . those flakes."

And that was it.

Miley couldn't believe it! She'd been duped! Foiled! Now she and Lilly were dead last on the list! She turned toward

Dandruff Danny's table. There was triumph in his eyes as he scratched his head, flakes flying through the air. Well, at least somebody was happy. That was worth something, right?

Right?

Chapter Eleven

Hannah Montana's record label had called twice that week to see if Mr. Stewart had written any new songs for Hannah's next album. He couldn't lose any more time.

As his grandfather used to say, "If you can't beat 'em, join 'em." In Mr. Stewart's case, it was more like, "If you can't beat 'em . . . feed 'em."

Mr. Dontzig and Oscar sat at the Stewarts' kitchen table, consuming the finest T-bone steak. Mr. Stewart had done the marinating, and now Jackson was doing the serving. He was even wearing a tuxedo.

Without the barking, Mr. Stewart had actually managed to finish a verse. He'd probably even be able to finish an entire song, if it weren't for Mr. Dontzig, whose yapping at the table was even worse than Oscar's yapping in the backyard.

"Next time, trim the fat," Mr. Dontzig ordered Mr. Stewart before turning to beam at his dog. "We've got our figures to worry about, don't we, Osky baby?"

Next time, Mr. Stewart decided, he'd serve them *two* steaks. After all, more chewing would mean less talking, and most important, less barking.

And then maybe he'd finally finish Hannah Montana's next big hit. . . .

HANNAH MONTANA

PART TWO

Chapter One

You never knew what was going to come out of Oliver's mouth. Or what he was going to put into it.

"Mmm . . ." Oliver said, squeezing gobs of mustard onto a piece of white bread, then licking his lips. He reminded Miley of her aunt's old dog, cleaning the kibble from his furry jowls. "Nothing better on a peanut-butter sandwich than pickle chips, a little bit of mustard, and chili."

Miley looked at Lilly. They both looked at Oliver. "What?" he demanded. "It all ends up in the same place." He took a large bite. Miley tried not to gag as chili juice dribbled down his chin.

A panicked scream came from across the cafeteria. Dandruff Danny was small in stature, but his voice sure could carry. Especially when he was panicked—which, in poor, beleaguered Dandruff Danny's case, was most of the time.

"Here she comes, here she comes!" he yelled. There was the screech of chairs being dragged along the linoleum floor as students huddled closer to one another for protection, then an overwhelming hush came over the room. "It's The Cracker!"

The cafeteria doors opened. A girl appeared. She wore a plaid shirt shredded at the shoulders, army-surplus pants, and combat boots.

Miley watched this arrival with interest. Okay, this wasn't your usual Malibu, California attire, but Miley was open-minded. As Hannah Montana, teen superstar, she was used to the folks who populated the entertainment industry, meaning she was used to all kinds of freaky quirks—especially where wardrobe was concerned.

"That's the new girl," Miley remarked. "Why do they call her The Cracker?"

"Watch," Oliver said ominously. As if on cue, The Cracker picked up a walnut and broke it open with her bare hands.

Lilly leaned in, eager to share what she knew. She was always up on the latest dirt. "Rumor is, when her old school kicked her out, they had to call animal control. It took six dog catchers and a giant net to bring her down."

Miley regarded this story skeptically. Not too long ago, she herself had been the new girl at school. She knew all too well how it felt to be alone in a new place. And it didn't help when people spread false, crazy stories about you. On Miley's first day, there'd been a rumor that she was such a hillbilly, she ate possum for dinner—raw! Of course, it turned out Oliver had started the rumor. As she watched him slobber over his disgusting sandwich, she marveled at how incredible it was that she'd ever forgiven him.

Miley's heart went out to the stranger. "I bet she's a nice kid," she said.

The Cracker busted open another nut, spraying shards of shell across the room.

". . . With freakishly strong hands," Lilly added.

Maybe Miley had been in Southern California for too long, but being mean to a new kid just felt like bad karma. "Come on, guys, I say we all go and say hi," she encouraged. "What do you know? She might surprise us."

Miley rose from her seat. Oliver and Lilly stayed glued to theirs. "Tell you what," Oliver suggested, "you go make friends with The Cracker, and I'll stay here and start writing your will."

"Ooh, put me down for all her shoes," Lilly quipped.

"Ah," said Miley, disappointed, "the fellowship of the weenies."

Apparently, she was on her own.

"Hi. I'm Miley." It seemed like a good place to start. She'd introduce herself, The Cracker would introduce herself. They'd say where they were from, talk about classes, and how much homework they had, maybe crack—*get it? crack?!*—a few jokes.

Except The Cracker said . . . nothing.

Hmm, time to try something else. Miley sat down at The Cracker's table. She noticed the metal lunch box the girl used. It looked like something a construction worker would carry—not your usual brown bag, but, hey, that was cool. Kind of retro, even.

Miley kept talking. "You know, I used to be new here, too."

Nothing.

The silence was unnerving. "But now I'm old here—well, not old-old, like this meatloaf." She pointed to the plate on The Cracker's table, then realized she'd just insulted the girl's lunch.

The Cracker used her palm to smash another nut. A piece of shell ricocheted off

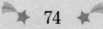

Miley's earlobe. *Ouch!* "Neat trick," Miley said enthusiastically. "You know, I saw *The Nutcracker* once. Loved it."

She barely knew what she was saying at this point, but apparently her ballet reference had worked to break the ice. The Cracker actually opened her mouth . . . and spoke. "Got any lipstick?" she asked. Hey, she even sounded friendly!

"Sure. Yeah!" Eagerly, Miley rummaged through her purse. She sure hoped she had something. At least a gloss. She dug through the mess of stray pens and empty candy wrappers. *Phew*, she found one. Persimmon Glaze by La Belle Fille. Miley had gotten it on Hannah Montana's last trip to Paris. It was a limited edition.

"This color will look great on you," Miley gushed. "I can tell we're gonna be good friends."

Not thirty seconds later, Miley shuffled back to her lunch table, a smushed lipstick in her hand and a dazed look in her eye. The Cracker had used the Persimmon Glaze . . . on Miley's face! Apparently, she'd decided it was time to try her hand at expressionist painting—using Miley's cheeks as her canvas. Her heart pounding, Miley had only three words to say as Lilly and Oliver gazed up at her in horror: "Call animal control."

So much for karma.

Chapter Two

Roxy was Miley's favorite bodyguard. So when it came time for her dad and Jackson to take their annual father-son fishing trip, she was psyched for Roxy to come stay at the house.

Not that Miley needed a babysitter; it was just that since she was also Hannah Montana, the Stewarts needed to take special precautions. Having Roxy around meant no paparazzi scares. It meant no uninvited fans. It also meant really good snacks and marathon sessions on the couch watching cheesy television. Roxy was the strongest person Miley had ever met, but she had a serious weakness for reality programming—especially shows with contestants eating live worms or doing death-defying stunts.

But this was really bad timing. Miley had been at The Cracker's mercy all day, and she was a wreck. It turned out the lipstick smackdown was only the beginning. It had been followed by the gym-uniform megawedgie; the glue-gun shoot-out in art class; and the locker-door slam dance. And poor Miley had been The Cracker's victim of choice every time!

If Roxy saw Miley like this, she'd go totally ballistic! It was Roxy's job to protect

Part One

"See you all next week, and we'll really pump up the party!" Miley, dressed as Hannah Montana, told the audience.

"I can make darn sure Amber never gets to sing with Hannah Montana," said Miley.

"Next time that dog barks, he's going to find out my woofer's bigger than his," said Jackson.

"Not only is she on the show, guess who gets to give her the good news?" Miley said.

Miley and her friends couldn't wait for Amber to humiliate herself on *Singing with the Stars*.

Miley, dressed as Hannah Montana, finished a rehearsal of "The Other Side of Me."

"You go through the red. She goes through the green—
because she's mean, like an evil queen," Lilly told Miley.

"I don't care what anybody else says. You're my real
friends. I'm sitting with you," said Oliver.

"Remember when I came here from Tennessee and *somebody* spread a rumor that I ate possum?" Miley said to her friends.

"You go make friends with The Cracker, and I'll stay here and start writing your will," Oliver said.

"The new kid in school—she thinks I look better with my hair up," Miley said.

"I don't have to *be* a puma, I just have to make The Cracker *think* I'm one," Miley told Lilly.

"The whole point of this trip was to have a little father-son bonding time. So we've hit a bump in the road," said Mr. Stewart.

"Roxy, what are you doing here?" Miley asked.

"Look who's coming this way. It's Troy McCann. He's so cute," said Lilly.

"I'll save you a seat in the cafeteria," said Roxy. "And I'll cut up your lunch into small, safe, non-chokeable pieces."

Miley, and Roxy took her job seriously. *Very* seriously.

Standing outside the front door to her house, Miley could hear Roxy on the phone to her dad. "I won't let anything harm a hair on your baby girl's pretty little head," Roxy was saying.

Well, that's ironic, Miley thought, because The Cracker's grand finale had been the hairiest—literally. She'd tied Miley's hands into her own hair.

Miley entered the house, lingering by the entranceway. Maybe she could run to her bedroom before Roxy caught a glimpse of her. Then again, she was helpless to do anything—she couldn't use her hands. But Roxy had eyes like an eagle and ears like a bat. No sooner had Miley exhaled than Roxy was standing before her and staring her down.

"Who did this to you?" she demanded, pulling Miley inside the living room.

"The new kid in school," Miley confessed. "She thinks I look better with my hair up."

Roxy looked appalled. "Didn't anybody try to help you?"

Lilly's weary voice came from behind Miley. Miley had been so distracted, she'd forgotten Lilly was with her. "That would be me." Apparently, The Cracker had gone for a doubleheader—Lilly had her hands tied to her hair, too.

Roxy saw no way around it. "First thing tomorrow," she instructed the girls, "you go right to that principal and tell him what's going on."

Miley couldn't believe her ears. "And be a snitch? No way!" She knew it had been a long time since Roxy was in school. Still, didn't she remember anything? There were rules! You couldn't just go tattle.

"Well, then it looks like I'm gonna have to go down there and protect you myself from The Cookie," Roxy said.

"She's not The Cookie, she's The Cracker," Miley explained.

"I don't care what kind of snack food she is, she's gonna have to get through me," Roxy declared.

This was exactly what Miley was afraid of. "Roxy, at school, I'm Miley, not Hannah," she reminded her. "I can't use my body-guard to fight my battles." Though, she had to admit, the thought of Roxy taking down The Cracker did have its appeal.

But maybe there was another way. Miley was always intending to sign up for a self-defense class. Maybe now was the time. In fact, Roxy could give her private lessons! "Can't you just teach me some of your special moves?" she asked.

"Oh, you mean like this?" Roxy loved an opportunity to show off her stuff. She flew through the kitchen, expertly jabbing and kicking at the air. She ended her display with a hiss.

"Roxy's like a puma." She growled. "And this kitty's got claws!" As if to prove her point, the pineapple on the kitchen counter collapsed into perfect quarters. Apparently, Roxy had sliced it in midair — she'd been so quick, Miley and Lilly had missed it.

Miley was impressed. "Can you teach me that?" she asked, imagining herself doing superhero stunts in the cafeteria.

"No way," Roxy told her. "You only use violence as a last resort."

Clearly, Roxy wasn't grasping how dire the situation was. "And when is that?" Miley asked sarcastically. "When she yanks out my intestine and wears it as a belt?!"

Roxy relented. "Okay, okay, I've got a move that'll work for you." She positioned herself in the center of the open floor. "Lilly," she instructed, "you be the bully, and I'll be Miley—now get all up in my grill."

Lilly was game, but she was also easily intimidated. She took two steps toward Roxy and lost her nerve. "I'd rather not," she said shyly.

"Come on, girl, show me what you got!" Roxy ordered.

Lilly summoned her courage. She strutted up to Roxy and did her best imitation of a bully. "Hey, Miley, give me your lipstick!"

Roxy threw her hands in the air and let out a hysterical shriek. "Principal! Principal!" she cried. "Help me! Help me!"

She turned to Miley with a smug look on her face. "*That's* how you handle the bully."

And here Miley thought she'd be learning some killer kung fu! Roxy was telling her to wimp out. "You want me to run away?" she asked incredulously.

"Like a free-range chicken," Roxy answered, then went upstairs to change. She'd gotten some pineapple juice on her shirt.

Now Miley and Lilly were alone in the kitchen, no closer to figuring out what to do. "I can't believe Roxy wouldn't show you some moves," Lilly said. "Just the way she puma'd that pineapple scared the juice out of me."

Miley thought for a moment. How to stop The Cracker? She already knew talking to her wouldn't work. It seemed like the only thing The Cracker would respond to was brute strength, and clearly Miley didn't have that. . . .

And then something clicked. Miley was an actress! Okay, officially she was a singer. But she'd taken acting classes. She'd appeared on an episode of *Zombie High*, the hit TV series. And being Hannah Montana onstage and Miley at school—well, really, she was acting all the time.

"Wait a minute, Lilly!" she exclaimed. "I don't have to *be* a puma, I just have to make The Cracker *think* I'm one."

She tried to do Roxy's signature hiss. It came out of her mouth sounding more like a purr. She'd have to work on that.

Chapter Three

This was California. Sure, the Stewarts had left the beach for the mountains. Still, it wasn't supposed to storm—and it certainly wasn't supposed to snow! Just Jackson's luck, it was doing both.

He hadn't even wanted to go on this father-son trip in the first place. Fishing? The only thing Jackson had ever caught fishing was a case of prickly heat. But his dad had insisted they needed some male-bonding time, and Jackson didn't have the heart to say no.

Still, he wondered why they couldn't have bonded in Malibu over hot dogs and soda. Or fish tacos—that was kind of like fishing, wasn't it? But no, his dad said they needed to get out of town, commune with nature, and be guys.

So here they were, more than an hour away from their destination, and the snow was piling up on either side of the freeway. Jackson suggested they turn around and go home. Mr. Stewart said it was too dangerous to go anywhere. They'd stay at a roadside motel and head out in the morning.

Easier said than done! The freeway was a long stretch of icy road and NO VACANCY signs. Jackson was just getting used to the idea of sleeping in the car when he spied a darkened clump of cabins with a broken sign advertising *V-C-N-C-Y*. They must have been out of the letter *A*. He told his dad to get off at the next exit.

The place was even more dilapidated than Jackson had imagined. Still, he was relieved to know they'd have a roof over their heads. Okay, it was a sagging, leaking roof, but it was a roof!

The motel manager's name was Gunther. "Well, I'm sorry 'bout your fishing trip," he drawled. "But that is why they call them freak storms—'cause they're freaky."

This guy was a slow talker. "C-c-c-could you open the door?" Jackson stammered. He was wearing his usual attire: a T-shirt and board shorts. They didn't offer much protection from the arctic weather they were experiencing.

Gunther looked at Jackson oddly, then

obliged. The old door hinges creaked. "Welcome to the honeymoon suite!" Gunther exclaimed.

Boy, was this room *not* what Jackson had expected! Pink carpet, red walls, a chandelier?! This was like a set out of one of the dorky romantic comedies Miley watched.

Mr. Stewart looked equally surprised by the surroundings. "Wow," was all he could muster.

"You know it's kinda funny," Jackson said, "when I pictured my honeymoon, it didn't include the big heart-shaped bed, or the red satin wallpaper, or my dad!"

"Well, it's better than having your mother-in-law along," said Gunther with a grimace. "That was a nightmare." Neither Mr. Stewart nor Jackson knew what to say to that. "Well, I'll tell ya what, I'll get

Franklin to bring you boys some fresh towelettes."

"You mean towels," Jackson corrected him. Come to think of it, he could sure use a hot shower.

"Okay," said Gunther with a shrug. He closed the door behind him.

Alone with his dad, Jackson got straight to the point. "I wanna go home."

Mr. Stewart smiled kindly at his son; still, he wasn't about to give him what he wanted. "Oh, come on, Jackson. The whole point of this trip was to have a little father-son bonding time."

Mr. Stewart flicked on what he thought was a light switch. A disco ball hanging from the ceiling spun as music blared. It was the kind of music that was supposed to be romantic. But it just put Jackson in a horrible mood!

As Mr. Stewart flicked on another switch, the bed started to rotate. He met Jackson's horrified expression. "So we've hit a bump in the road," he said. "Why don't we just look at it as an adventure?"

Adventure, Jackson thought derisively. That's one word for it.

Chapter Four

Some people cracked their knuckles to release tension. The Cracker cracked her neck. She turned her head from right to left, taking great pride in the way the *criccckkkk* sound echoed down the school hallway.

Miley and Lilly watched from an unseen corner. As intimidating as The Cracker's showmanship was, Miley couldn't let it bug her. Now was her chance to stop the bully once and for all.

She counted down in her head. Ten, nine, eight, seven . . .

She got her feet into position. Six, five, four . . .

She raised her fists in the air. And . . . three, two, one!

Miley took off with Lilly by her side.

Moments later, they stood face to face with The Cracker. Miley's lip curled into a snarl, as she raised her fists and judo-chopped.

"Hi-ya!" she screamed. She did Roxy's signature scissor kick. "Hi-yo!" A double chop, with a backward spin. "Hi-ya-ya-ya-ya-ya!"

She'd been expecting some sort of reaction. A whimper maybe. Perhaps even a look of shock. But it was just like the day before, when she was trying to be friendly. The Cracker just stared at her blankly.

"That's right, Miley, like a puma!" Miley growled. "Hi-ya!" She was putting on an unbelievable performance—if she did say so herself.

Still . . . nothing.

Lilly chimed in. "Ooh, yeah, she's a baaaad puma!" She roared. "You better run, Cracker!"

The Cracker didn't move.

"Go ahead, start running. . . ."

Nothing.

Lilly turned to Miley. "Why isn't she running?"

At which point, The Cracker stepped toward them. Miley and Lilly stepped away.

"I'm warning you—Miley like a puma." Miley was saying the words, but she was starting to doubt them. "Miley like a puma." Her voice wavered. She threw in another "Hi-ya!" for good measure.

The Cracker leaned in closer. Their noses were an inch apart. They were so close, Miley could smell the walnuts on The Cracker's breath.

Miley might be brave, but she wasn't dumb. "Miley run like a puma!" she yelped, backing away. She pulled Lilly toward the bathroom. The Cracker was after them!

Miley and Lilly had always wondered what it'd be like to be twins. But they'd never wondered what it'd be like to be constantly joined at the hip. Now, with their hair tied together, courtesy of The Cracker, they were getting a taste of it—and it was going to take some getting used to.

"Ow!" yelped Lilly.

"Talk about a hairy situation," Miley grumbled.

"Don't make me laugh," Lilly moaned.

❄ ❄ ❄

Dandruff Danny came tearing down the hall. "Run for your lives!" he warned everyone. "She's coming!"

Miley happened to know for a fact that The Cracker wasn't coming down the hall. She was in the cafeteria eating lunch. Apparently, torturing people caused you to work up an appetite — Miley had heard the bully's stomach rumbling during their most recent en*tangle*-ment.

"Danny, calm down," she said, "you're flaking up the hall." With her own scalp stinging, she had newfound sympathy for Dandruff Danny's affliction.

"Not The Cracker!" Dandruff Danny cried. "There's a new girl in school! She's even scarier!"

This Miley and Lilly had to see. Scarier than The Cracker? Did such a thing even exist? A bold voice was coming from around the corner.

"Where is she?!" the voice demanded.

Boy, it sounded familiar.

"Where's The Cracker?!"

"Wait a minute," said Lilly, "that sounds like . . ."

"Oh, no," Miley moaned. Could it be? Was it really? Yes, it was. . . .

Chapter Five

. . . Roxy.

"What up, girls?! Where do I park my board?" Miley had seen Roxy go undercover tons of times before. But she'd never seen her dressed as a high school student — or how Roxy thought a high school student would dress. Miley wondered how Roxy had done her research. Maybe she'd spent the morning watching old sitcoms set in high school, because her look was wildly out of date.

"Roxy, what are you doing here?" Miley knew Roxy would be the last person to spill her secret. Still, she couldn't help feeling nervous. Roxy was from Hannah Montana World. School, on the other hand, was Miley Stewart World. She needed to keep the two as separate as possible. "You can't be here."

Roxy wasn't hearing it. "You said you weren't going to the principal, and you're not wearing your running shoes."

Miley glanced at her feet. Roxy had a point: running shoes would have come in handy when The Cracker was chasing her and Lilly. Then again, her new flip-flops were so cute! Plus, they went perfectly with her skirt.

"If you won't protect yourself, Roxy will," her bodyguard went on. "Now stand still, it's time to pick this problem apart. Turn around."

She pulled a couple of hair picks from her back pocket, and hacked at Miley and Lilly's heads. Not only did she separate them, she gave them each a stylin' new do.

"Wow, your hair looks great," Lilly told Miley, amazed.

"You, too," Miley said. "I love the braid." A braid! How did Roxy do it?

"That's my signature," Roxy boasted. "Now come on, this puma's hungry for some Cracker."

Well, if Roxy was going to be at school, she might as well do what she came to do. Miley and Lilly showed her the way.

Roxy didn't waste any time. She went right up to The Cracker and shouted in her face, "You're sitting in my seat."

The Cracker rose from her seat in disbelief. Who dared to challenge her reign of terror? "I don't think so," she replied, smashing a nut in her fist to prove her point.

Roxy wasn't impressed. "Cute," she countered. "But can you do this?" A baseball player was sitting at the next table. Roxy grabbed the ball from his mitt and threw it in the air. She caught it and squeezed, so that when she released her grip, all she was holding was a palmful of dust.

"I'm not scared of you," The Cracker said, matching Roxy's glare with an angry one of her own.

Next, came what Miley and Lilly would later refer to as The Great Cafeteria Stare Down.

The Cracker stared at Roxy. Roxy stared at The Cracker.

The Cracker started to fidget. Roxy stared at The Cracker.

The Cracker began to tremble. Roxy stared at The Cracker.

The Cracker looked uneasy. Roxy stared at The Cracker.

The Cracker barreled out of the cafeteria without even looking back! Miley couldn't believe it! The Cracker had . . . cracked!

"What'd you do?" Lilly was practically reeling in astonishment.

"ESP," Roxy answered. "Extrasensory Puma."

Chapter Six

Just when Jackson thought the father-son weekend couldn't get any lamer—or creepier—it turned out Gunther was a ventriloquist! He had a wooden dummy named Franklin who "worked" as the bellhop. And the maid. He even performed the nightly turndown. Jackson had never seen a wooden dummy try to fluff a pillow before, and he hoped he'd never see it again.

Franklin's appearances marked only the beginning of what would turn out to be a very rough night. Between the freezing cold air whistling outside the rattling windows and Mr. Stewart's boar-like snoring, Jackson had trouble falling asleep. He tossed and turned until the sun came up. Only then did he close his eyes. Jackson dreamed that he was snug in his bed at home, waking up to the warm Malibu sunshine streaming into his room.

Instead, he arose to Gunther wheeling a rickety dining cart into the room. He was delivering the "deluxe complimentary breakfast" into the honeymoon suite.

If Gunther's idea of "deluxe" was generic cereal and individual coffee creamers, Jackson thought, he'd hate to see what he considered "standard."

"Thank you, but we're not going to be

needing any of that . . . yummy looking breakfast," Mr. Stewart told the manager. "We're gonna go ahead and see if we can't salvage what's left of this fishing trip."

Salvage their fishing trip! Sheesh! Jackson was hoping his dad would call the whole trip a wash. He wanted to go home! Then again, he'd rather be baiting worms on a fishing hook than hanging out in the honeymoon suite of doom.

"Oh, I don't think that's gonna happen today," Gunther told them. "The roads are still snowed in. Looks to me like you're stuck."

He opened the front door to leave. A bank of snow blocked him. "What do you know about that?" Gunther shrugged. "Looks like we're all stuck."

Being stuck in this creepy motel room with his dad was one thing. Being stuck in this creepy motel room with his dad *and* *Gunther* was another. Still, Jackson was determined to look on the bright side.

"At least he doesn't have the dummy," Jackson whispered to Mr. Stewart.

"Who you calling a dummy, dummy?" came a voice from under the breakfast cart.

Uh-oh.

Tons of snow. A creepy motel room. A weird proprietor. And a wooden dummy. This scene had "horror flick" written all over it. "Dad," Jackson whispered, "I've seen this movie before—and you and I don't make it to the sequel!"

An hour later, Jackson was beginning to feel even more hopeless. In fact, he was downright hysterical. "We're never getting out. We're gonna die in here!" he wailed.

Usually, Mr. Stewart thought, it was his

daughter who was the drama queen. "No one is going to die," he told Jackson. "Now stop focusing on the negative and focus on the positive. The snowplow will be here soon." He nodded toward Gunther, who had finally managed to get the city's snow-removal department on the line.

Unfortunately, the call didn't go so well. "Bad news, fellas," he said, hanging up the phone. "Plow won't be here till morning."

"Sweet frozen niblets!" Mr. Stewart exclaimed.

Jackson couldn't take it anymore. How could his dad be so cavalier? *Sweet frozen niblets?!* With twenty-four hours to go, this situation called more for an eardrum-piercing, *"Aaaaahhh!"* He ran to the door and threw himself against it. "I want to live!" he shouted. "I want to live! I want to live!"

Usually, Jackson was the last person to volunteer for outdoor chores. But now he was ready to dig them out of the room with his bare hands.

No, forget that, it would take too long. He had a better idea.

"I'm gonna ram it!" he announced. He opened the door and faced the giant drift of snow. "See you on the other side, old man!" he told his dad.

Jackson took a few steps back and geared up. Sure, it was going to be cold. But it would be worth it. He took a deep breath and hit the ice running. *Crrrrr-ack!*

And then his arms and feet were moving, but he wasn't. The snow was too deep. He was stuck.

"I can't feel my lips," he said, his teeth chattering.

Chapter Seven

Miley couldn't believe how wrong she'd been. Having Roxy lurking around the school's hallways wasn't bad at all. In fact, it was awesome! Every time The Cracker tried something, Roxy was ready for her. Miley and Lilly could finally relax, let down their guard, and be normal again.

Miley had to hand it to The Cracker—the girl didn't give up easily. Roxy had foiled her every bullying move that morning, yet

The Cracker kept trying. That afternoon, the bully found Lilly and Miley in the hallway and, when she didn't see Roxy nearby, made her move.

Luckily, Roxy had a way of showing up at exactly the right time. Before The Cracker could lift a hand toward Miley, Roxy was there to stop her. "Don't even think about it," she warned The Cracker. "In fact, don't even think about thinking about it."

Miley nodded in satisfaction as The Cracker shuffled off, cowering. "Life at school just got a whole lot better."

Lilly agreed. "Tell me about it. Look who's coming this way. It's Troy McCann. He's so cute."

It suddenly dawned on Miley that ever since The Cracker had shown up at school, Miley's main focus had been escaping her clutches. Thank goodness for Roxy. Now Miley could focus on more important things, including boys!

"Hey, Lilly. Hey, Miley." With his hair swooping across his eyes, Troy McCann was looking especially cute today. "Listen, the basketball team is having a party this Saturday, and I was wondering if you guys want to go."

Perfect! Usually, Miley had gigs on Saturday night, but this weekend was free and clear.

"No, we can't," Roxy replied grimly.

What? Miley and Lilly couldn't believe it!

Troy looked as surprised as Miley and Lilly. "Actually, I—"

Roxy didn't like repeating herself. "I said, no," she huffed. "Now move, move, move!"

Once he was gone, she turned to Miley and Lilly. "Seems like a sweet boy," she remarked, adding darkly, "those are the ones you've got to watch."

"Roxy, what are you doing?" Lilly asked. "I've had my eyes on him."

Roxy ignored her. "I never realized how many dangers lurk in these halls. Bullies, boys—and that chicken potpie they served today? That was nasty."

Roxy had a look in her eyes that Miley didn't like. "You're not thinking of staying, are you, Roxy?" she asked hesitantly.

"I have to," Roxy answered with resolve. "If I leave, The Cracker's going to go back to cracking. And since you won't go to the principal, I've got to be here to protect you."

Miley could see her high school future pass before her eyes—and it was dismal. She could live without the chicken potpie and the bullies. But boys? What was high school without that? Not to mention feeling free to do whatever you wanted without being watched. It struck Miley that if she were Hannah Montana full-time, this would be what her life would always be like. And that kind of a life . . . wasn't a life.

When it came to the blazing California sun, you could never protect yourself enough. But when it came to Roxy, sometimes even a little protection was just too much.

The question was: what to do about it?

Chapter Eight

At least they had TV. Okay, yeah, the only channels that came in were the ones in Spanish, and neither Jackson nor Mr. Stewart spoke Spanish.

Still, it was either watch shows in a foreign language or watch Gunther and Franklin napping in the armchair. And Gunther drooled. Jackson picked the Spanish soap operas.

"*Maria, tu eres mi corazon.*" Jackson had

no idea what Pablo was saying, but he knew it was sincere.

"*Pablo, podemos nunca ser juntos.*" He had no idea what Maria was saying, either. But he was pretty sure Pablo didn't deserve it.

"Poor Pablo," he said. "She's breaking his heart."

Mr. Stewart shook his head mournfully. "Why do they always go for the bad hombres?"

Jackson looked at the clock. Whoa! It was already afternoon. They'd been watching Maria and Pablo for hours, but it felt like minutes. Wait, Jackson thought, didn't time only go fast when you were having fun? Hadn't he read that on an embroidered pillow at his grandmother's house? Could it be that he was actually—shock of all shocks—having fun?! He glanced over at his dad who was staring tearfully at the screen. "Hey, Dad. Look at us. We're bonding."

Mr. Stewart had been thinking the same thing. "You're right, son," he said. "And now that we have, let's get the heck out of here."

"I'd love to," Jackson replied, "but where's the snowplow?"

"There is no snowplow," a voice said. It came from Franklin's mouth.

"Gunther?" Mr. Stewart said, staring at the hotel manager. But Gunther appeared to be fast asleep.

"No, it's Franklin," the wooden dummy answered. "Gunther's asleep."

Jackson shuddered. He could practically *hear* the trills of horror-movie music in the background.

"Don't worry 'bout it, son," Mr. Stewart

told Jackson, though he sounded a little worried himself. "He's probably just talking in his sleep."

Franklin interrupted them — and not very politely. "Oh! Good work, Einstein. Now shut your yapper and listen. He never did call for a snowplow. But there's a heater register right behind the nightstand. You can open it and get to your car."

Careful not to wake Gunther, Mr. Stewart went toward the nightstand. The dummy was right. Who'd have thought? "C'mon," he told Jackson. "We're going home."

Sweeter words Jackson had never heard! He grabbed his duffel bag and started out without looking back.

Then that other, creepy voice piped up again. "Take me with you," said Franklin. Jackson and Mr. Stewart stopped in their tracks.

"Okay, Dad, I know this is weird, but . . ." Jackson couldn't believe what he was about to say. ". . . in a strange way, he did save our lives."

"Listen to yourself, son," Mr. Stewart protested. "He's a doll."

"Dad, in some part of his brain, Gunther wants us to do this."

"But it's stealing. . . . I think," Mr. Stewart said.

"Just leave fifty bucks on the table," Franklin told them. "He got me at a garage sale for five."

That sounded fair enough. Mr. Stewart placed a bill on the nightstand as Jackson gingerly picked the dummy off of the sleeping Gunther and carried him through the vent to liberation.

Mr. Stewart and Jackson were in the car before Gunther opened his eyes back in the motel room. "Works every time," he said slyly before pocketing Mr. Stewart's crisp fifty.

They'd been conned, but they would never know it. Anyway, a good father-son bonding session was worth way more than fifty bucks.

Chapter Nine

It was one thing for Roxy to impose security restrictions on Miley. It was another thing for her to impose *wardrobe* restrictions. Especially when they involved nurse's shoes. Nurse's shoes! Squishy-heeled, lace-up, orthopedic nurse's shoes! Roxy claimed they were the safest soles to wear on the school's linoleum floors. Skid-proof, she called them. Style-proof was more like it.

Then again, the nurse's shoes were the

least of Miley's wardrobe problems today. That morning, she'd assembled an awesome ensemble: white hoodie, jeans, red tank top, cute beads. She'd gone down to breakfast and discovered Roxy wearing the exact same thing! They were twins! Identical twins! It was embarrassing!

"She's impossible," Miley complained to Lilly. "I can't talk to boys, and these nurse's shoes are hideous, and now she's making us wear the same clothes so if I get lost, she can tell people—" She cleared her throat, then did her best Roxy imitation. "—I'm looking for someone dressed just like this."

"Hey, only four more years and you can wear what you want. Unless she follows you to college." If Lilly was trying to make Miley feel better, it wasn't working.

"Why didn't I tell the principal in the first place?" Miley groaned. "Sure, I would've been a snitch, but I would've been a snitch without a computer tracking device."

"Say what?"

Miley pointed to the GPS-equipped hair clip Roxy had forced her to wear that morning. "It's in my barrette!"

"Well, it's too late to tell the principal," Lilly pointed out. "Now that Roxy is here, The Cracker isn't bullying anybody anymore."

Roxy was so stealthy, Miley never heard her coming. At that very moment, she seemed to appear out of thin air. "I'll save you a seat in the cafeteria," she told the girls. "And I'll cut up your lunch into small, safe, non-chokeable pieces," she told Miley.

"Great," said Miley, whose chipper tone only barely masked her utter dread. They couldn't go on like this. Soon Roxy would be hand-feeding her lunch and running security checks on the librarians. Something had to change. And the only person who could make it change was Miley. It was time to fight her own battles.

And that gave her an idea. . . .

"Wait a minute," she said to her friend. "Lilly, what would happen if Roxy wasn't here anymore?"

Well, that was an easy one. "The Cracker would bust you like a piñata, and she'd probably use Dandruff Danny as the stick," Lilly answered.

Strangely, that was just what Miley was hoping she'd say. "Perfect!" she exclaimed.

Lilly was understandably confused. Did Miley *want* The Cracker to destroy her? "Am I missing something?"

Miley wouldn't explain. "Just meet me in the cafeteria with the principal in five minutes," she said.

"What about Roxy?" Lilly asked.

Good point. Miley reached into her hair and unclipped the barrette. "Hey, Jeanie," she called out to the first person she saw. "This barrette would look perfect in your light brown hair."

"Thanks, Miley," said Jeanie, happy to have a new accessory. She fastened the barrette and headed off.

Miley pushed Lilly toward the principal's office, then ducked into the bathroom. Just in time. A confounded Roxy was hot on Jeanie's trail. "Where is that girl going?" she muttered, staring at the GPS coordinates on her PDA screen. "We don't have gym this period."

It wouldn't take long before Roxy figured out what Miley had done. She had to work fast.

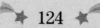

Chapter Ten

Miley paced the hall impatiently as she awaited Lilly's call. The clock was ticking. She figured Roxy had probably followed Jeanie into the girl's locker room and was scouting the place for signs of Miley. Miley had set her phone to vibrate, and when it finally jittered in her hand, she almost dropped it—probably because she was feeling a little skittish herself.

"Okay, I've got the principal," Lilly reported to her, "and we're coming down the hall right now!"

"Great," Miley said, gearing herself up. "The fox is on the move."

"Wow, somebody thinks a lot of themselves," Lilly commented.

What could Miley say? She had a weakness for corny spy-movie lingo. It got her in the mood. "It means I'm going in!" she snapped before hanging up.

Funny that in her plot to get rid of Roxy, Miley was using the very tactics that Roxy had taught her. She entered the cafeteria and scanned the room, quickly taking stock of who was around: there were the jocks at the table by the window; there were Amber and Ashley on line for frozen yogurt; there was Dandruff Danny, dining solo.

Most important, there was The Cracker

hunched over her metal lunch box, devouring a sandwich.

Dandruff Danny had taken a special liking to Roxy, whose mere presence at school had provided him with a level of protection he'd never dreamed possible. Miley made sure The Cracker was in earshot when she sat down at Dandruff Danny's table.

"I have some bad news," Miley said somberly. "Roxy arm-wrestled the principal and accidentally snapped his wrist like a twig. He kicked her out of school."

Poor Dandruff Danny. Miley hated to scare him. But using him as a pawn was a necessary evil in order to accomplish a greater good.

"Roxy got expelled?!" Dandruff Danny's voice cracked, and his hands started to tremble. "I'm doomed!" He stood up, his legs wobbling. For a brief second, Miley thought the poor kid might faint. Instead, he bolted from the cafeteria, arms flailing in panic.

Miley had been expecting this. It was part of her plan. Still, she cringed fearfully when she felt The Cracker's meaty finger-tips on her shoulder. Here we go, she thought, turning to face the bully.

"Sorry to hear about your friend." Somehow, The Cracker managed to grin and sneer at the same time.

"Yeah, I'm helpless now," Miley teased. Any second now, Lilly and the principal would appear.

Any second now . . .

What was taking them so long?

Any second now . . .

Lilly? Lilly?

Aaaaahhh!

* * *

Miley had a difficult time opening her eyes—after all, she had clumps of ranch dressing in her eyelashes. There was Thousand Island in her right ear, creamy Italian in her left. And was that shredded lettuce in her left nostril? Yuck!

Boy, The Cracker worked fast! Before Miley knew it, she'd been hoisted into the air, carted across the cafeteria, and dumped on top of the salad bar.

Then The Cracker had gone artistic again—Miley was still the canvas, only this time salad fixings were The Cracker's palette.

After dousing Miley with dressing, she'd showered her with bacon bits and garlic croutons. She'd filled Miley's socks with chickpeas and squeezed tomatoes in her hair.

The Cracker rubbed her hands together

gleefully as an audience of onlookers gaped at the spectacle before them.

"Looks pretty good," The Cracker boasted to the crowd, "but it still needs something. Oh, yeah, nuts." She grabbed a handful and started smashing.

Ouch! A hailstorm of crumbling nuts and shells hit Miley in the face. She turned toward the salad bar's glass wall to shield herself and caught a glimpse of Lilly walking toward her. It was about time!

"I'm late, aren't I?" asked Lilly.

"Just a smidge," quipped Miley, who would have been angry if she weren't so relieved to see rescue in sight. Not only was Lilly there to see what The Cracker had just done. The principal was with her.

Chapter Eleven

"**Y**ou did the right thing coming to me, girls. She's not going to bother anyone else in the school again," the principal said. He gave The Cracker a stern look. "You have anything to say for yourself, young lady?"

"Sorry, Stewart," The Cracker muttered to Miley, though she obviously didn't mean it.

"That's okay," said Miley, though she obviously didn't mean it, either.

"All right, Henrietta Laverne," the principal said, shaking his head in disappointment. "Let's go."

"Henrietta Laverne?" Lilly gaped. She and Miley didn't even try to contain their laughter.

As Miley watched The Cracker leave the cafeteria for good, she had a brief moment of sympathy for the bully who'd made her life a nightmare. The Cracker sure had a lot of energy—if only she would use it for something good. She was so angry. Then again, with a name like Henrietta Laverne, who could blame her?

"At least now we know why she's so mean," Miley said with a shrug.

Just then, Roxy sauntered into the cafeteria. In all the hullabaloo, Miley had forgotten the whole point of what she'd been trying to do—get Roxy off the campus!

Now it was time to break the news that her services were no longer needed.

Luckily, Roxy took her dismissal surprisingly well. "Thank goodness that's over," she groaned, slumping into a chair at the lunch table. "I was running out of fake dangers to protect you from."

"Excuse me?" Miley gasped. What was Roxy talking about?

"Oh, I only did all that stuff to make your life so miserable that you'd go to the principal like you should've in the first place," Roxy explained.

It took Miley several seconds to absorb what her bodyguard had just said. "So this was your plan from the beginning?" She couldn't believe it! She'd been played.

"That's right. You've heard of reverse psychology? Well, welcome to reverse

Roxology!" Roxy grinned. "No need to thank me, honey."

"Wait a minute." Miley was still trying to process this information. "I got tossed around like a salad, so you could teach me a lesson?"

"You never do eat your vegetables," Roxy pointed out.

Miley was tired. Her body ached from being crammed into the salad bar. And the lingering scent of garlic croutons was making her queasy. Still, she was pretty sure that if she really tried, she could take Roxy.

"Well you better run!" she warned her favorite bodyguard. "Miley like a puma!" She clawed viciously at the air as Roxy tore off, laughing.

Now Miley was laughing, too. She zipped out of the cafeteria and zoomed down the hallway, going as fast as her nursing shoes could take her.

Put your hands together for the next Hannah Montana book . . .

Adapted by Heather Alexander

Based on the series created by Michael Poryes and Rich Correll & Barry O'Brien

Based on the episode, "Money For Nothing, Guilt For Free," Written by Heather Wordham

Miley Stewart slid into her seat behind her best friend, Lilly Truscott. She glanced up at the school clock. Four more hours to go—two hundred and forty minutes.

Miley couldn't wait for school to be over.

She and Lilly were planning to do some serious shopping that afternoon.

"Okay, I want everyone to close your eyes and find your happy place," said Miley's teacher, Mr. Corelli. He nodded his head enthusiastically.

Miley glanced around the room. All of her classmates had shut their eyes. She shrugged and figured she'd log some beauty z's, too. She closed her eyes.

"Now imagine all the good things in your life," Mr. Corelli continued.

That was easy! She thought of hanging out with her friends at the beach, playing her guitar, and singing in front of a cheering crowd as pop star Hannah Montana.

Miley smiled to herself. The kids at school would flip if they ever found out that teen music sensation Hannah Montana was really Miley Stewart. Only her best friends and family were in on her secret.

Miley was suddenly broken out of her reverie by the sound of a loud voice.

"Great shoes, perfect hair," Ashley Dewitt crooned. Miley frowned, but kept her eyes closed and tried to concentrate.

"Very Berry lip shine!" cried Amber Addison, Ashley's best friend.

"Oooh!" the two girls squealed.

Miley didn't have to open her eyes to know what would happen next. Amber and Ashley reached across the aisle and touched pointer fingers. *"Sssss!"* they hissed, as if they were burning hot.

"Wow!" Lilly whispered to Miley. "Even though I can't see it, it's still annoying."

Miley kept her eyes closed and nodded. "I know. Now it's in *my* happy place."

"Okay, open your eyes," Mr. Corelli instructed.

Miley looked at her teacher. Today he was wearing a red vest and, of course, a bow tie. Mr. Corelli wore a bow tie every day.

"Now that you have had time to think about what you have, it's time to think about those who aren't as lucky," said Mr. Corelli. "Yes, it's time again for our school to raise money for . . ." He faked a drum roll. ". . . the United People's Relief Fund. And you, my little relievers, are going to help the less fortunate."

"Like Ms. Dawson, the librarian?" Miley's other best friend, Oliver Oken, called from the desk behind her.

"Ms. Dawson is not less fortunate. She chooses to dress that way. It's too bad. She could be all that and a bowl of pudding," Mr. Corelli said dreamily.

Just then, the classroom door swung open, and Miley's classmate Sarah rushed in.

"I'm sorry I'm late, Mr. Corelli," she said, out of breath. She pushed her glasses higher up her nose. "I was on my way to school when I had to wrestle a cat away from a baby bird, and then I felt sorry for the cat, so I went to the pet store to get him some food, and then I saw this lost dog with a sore paw—"

Mr. Corelli held up his hands, as if in surrender. "Whoa, Sarah!"

Miley had known Sarah for years, and she was always doing something to help others.

Mr. Corelli looked at Sarah and sighed. "Why is it every time I talk to you I get the urge to give blood and call my mom? Which, if you knew my mom, is sort of the same thing." He pointed Sarah toward her desk. "I'm sorry," he said to the class. "Where were we?"

"You were crushing on Ms. Dawson," Miley called out helpfully.

"Ewww!" Lilly cried.

"No, I wasn't," Mr. Corelli corrected Miley. "I was thinking about pudding." His stomach growled loudly. "Moving on. United People's Relief. Like last year, the person or team that raises the most *ka-ching* gets the day off of school, their picture in the newspaper, and a three-hundred-dollar gift card to the Malibu Mall—"

The school bell rang loudly. Kids leaped out of their chairs and headed toward the door. Mr. Corelli didn't mind. "Finally! Lunch time!" he cried.

Lilly turned toward Miley. "We *have* to win. I need a new deck for my skateboard."

"I just want to win so Amber and Ashley don't," Miley said. "Otherwise, it's going to be another year of listening to them gloat."

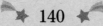

She wrinkled her nose. Amber and Ashley had won last year, and they were *still* reminding everyone at school.

"Hey, guys," Amber said. She and Ashley stopped at Miley's and Lilly's desks. "We know we gloated last year, and we feel really bad about that."

"So we just wanted to say good luck," Ashley added as she patted Miley on the back. Amber nodded and patted Lilly on the back. "May the best fund-raiser win," Ashley continued. Then she and Amber skipped out the door.

"Okay, something doesn't smell right here," Miley announced.

Lilly grimaced. "Sorry. I knew I shouldn't have had that breakfast burrito."

"No, I'm talking about Amber and Ashley. They're up to something, and we just have to watch our backs."

"You got it," Lilly said. She followed her friend out of the classroom.

Between classes, the halls of Seaview were like the mall the day before Christmas—packed. Some kids pushed and shoved to get to their lockers. Some walked by in an aimless daze. But today, Miley noticed, kids were whispering even more than usual. . . .